T3745d

Don't Forget Michael

By the Same Author
Brother of the Wolves

Don't Forget Michael

JEAN THOMPSON
illustrated by Margot Apple

William Morrow and Company
New York 1979

Library of Congress Cataloging in Publication Data

Thompson, Jean, 1933-
   Don't forget Michael.

   Summary: Four episodes in which seven-year-old Michael copes with being the smallest and quietest in a large, clamorous family.
   [1. Family life—Fiction]   I. Apple, Margot.   II. Title.
PZ7.T371595Do   [E]   79-16637
ISBN 0-688-22196-3
ISBN 0-688-32196-8 lib. bdg.

Printed in the United States of America.
2   3   4   5   6   7   8   9   10

In memory of my parents-in-law,
Selma and Clint Thompson, Sr.

Contents

Misplaced Michael

Michael was the smallest of all the McBrides. He sometimes felt lost in the middle of his own big family. Everyone else was taller than he was, even his sister Connie, who was next older. She was tall for her age and he was short, so it seemed that everyone else was always laughing and talking over his head while he stood way down below, completely forgotten. Besides being short, he was also quiet. Everyone else had a lot to say, and they were inclined to say it in loud voices. Michael had quite a lot to say, too, except never as fast or as loud as the rest of them, so usually nobody seemed to hear the things he did say.

Towering over him were Mom and Dad and his tall brothers: Timothy, Kevin, and Shawn. Besides Connie, there was another older sister named Heather. They were just the people who lived in the same house with him. There were a lot of other McBrides who lived in different houses. They visited each other often, and they did almost everything together.

There were Grandma and Grandpa McBride. There were four pairs of McBride uncles and aunts and Uncle Bob, who wasn't married. The uncles and aunts who were married had thirteen children divided up among them.

That was only half of the family. Mom's relatives were named Cameron, and there were a lot of them, too, starting with Grandma Cameron and Great-Aunt Olivia. Then there were four

Cameron pairs of uncles and aunts and a dozen cousins.

Each family had a variety of pets. Michael's family had two dogs, named Muffin and Chipper, and a cat called Midnight. There was a hamster—Hamlet, of course—and a rabbit named Fuzzy. Grandma Cameron had a crabby parrot called Captain Kidd that had belonged to Grandpa Cameron before he died. The parrot had spent many years watching baseball games on TV with Grandpa. The only words he would say were, "Ball four. Take a walk," and "Strike three. You're out."

There were so many other pets that the McBrides and the Camerons couldn't keep them straight. Sometimes they even got the human cousins confused.

Great-Aunt Olivia was always calling Michael Matthew. Matthew was Aunt Julia and Uncle Terry's son. She called Matthew Michael, too. At first Michael would say, "I'm not Matthew. I'm Michael," and Matthew would say, "I'm not Michael. I'm Matthew." But pretty soon they both gave up and answered to either name. Sometimes they pretended to be each other on purpose, and sometimes they could fool Aunt Hilary and Uncle John, too. They did look a lot alike.

Today they were all going on a picnic. Grandma and Grandpa McBride came early to help load the car. They put in fried chicken, potato salad, and Grandma's extra-double-chocolate cake made from her special secret recipe that she promised she would write down someday. They stuffed in suntan oil, baseballs, mitts, old cushions, and campstools to sit on.

The rest of the McBrides and Camerons arrived in one packed car after another. At last they were ready to go. All the people, most of the dogs, and even a couple of cats squeezed back into the cars. Grandma Cameron brought along Captain Kidd. She said sunshine and fresh air were as good for him as they were for anyone, and, besides, he was even grouchier than usual if he was left alone.

The cars trundled along in a procession, and everyone waved and yelled back and forth at everyone else. The dogs barked out the windows, and Captain Kidd shrieked, "Strike three. You're out."

When they came to the picnic spot, McBrides and Camerons tumbled out of their cars like clowns at a circus. They spread out cloths and put food on the tables. Some started a game of five hundred in the field. Some dashed into the woods and played cowboys and Indians with much whooping and shouting among the trees. The radios blared. Mom and Uncle Bob danced by the cars while Dad and Grandpa clapped and whistled. The dogs barked and raced around. Captain Kidd hung in his cage under a tree with his back turned to everybody.

Michael played ball and yelled and cheered with everyone else. He played cowboy and whooped and shot *bang bang* as loudly as anyone. He ate. Twice. He waded in the creek and splashed and shrieked along with the rest. By then he was very tired and his ears rang. He felt that if he heard any more noise, he was going to short out like a computer on TV, lights flashing wildly on and off, sparks flying out, and finally grind to a stop.

He staggered off up the creek, and the sounds grew fainter behind him. After a while he found a nice mossy spot behind a log, and he lay down and fell asleep.

When he woke up, he started back to the picnic. People shouted and car doors slammed. Engines throbbed, gears clashed and meshed together. He could hear Captain Kidd screeching, "You're out. You're out."

"See you next week," Dad yelled, and the engines roared louder.

Were they leaving already? Michael started to run, splashing through the water, pushing aside the bushes. By the time he got to the picnic ground, the cars were already far down the road, going off like a gypsy caravan.

"Wait! Wait!" Michael shouted, but they were too far away for anyone to hear him. Through the rear window of the last car, he saw Cousin Charles pounding on Cousin Walter. Both mouths were open, and he guessed they were yelling. They turned the corner and went out of sight.

They had left him. He was all alone. His family's forgetting him was positively the worst thing that had ever happened to him in his entire life. He couldn't remember ever being completely alone before, not even once. Somebody was always with him, and now there wasn't anybody.

He knew he was going to cry, even though he was seven years old. A big lump filled his throat. Tears rose up behind his eyes, ready to pour down his cheeks. He drew in his breath with a hiccup, all set to sob.

Before he could make a sound, he noticed something funny. There was something in his ears that had never been there before. He held his breath and listened. There was silence.

That was all. There was nothing else. No Kevin yelling at Connie or Timothy pretending he was revving up his imaginary motorcycle. His mother wasn't whistling. His father wasn't mowing the grass. Heather wasn't practicing her tap steps, clopping like a rhythmic horse around the kitchen floor. Muffin and Chipper weren't barking, and Midnight wasn't meowing because no one had fed him.

Michael had never heard total silence before. He was amazed how quiet it could be. His ears seemed to stretch and expand, reaching out into the silence around him. Then he heard a tiny whirring sound.

A big green grasshopper went sailing past his shoulder and landed on the grass beyond. Michael walked toward it, and the grasshopper whirred off a few more feet. Michael followed. What a neat little noise it made, so tiny and yet so busy.

He followed the rustling flight until he heard another sound. This one was soft and gentle, too— the silvery sound of water running over pebbles. He lay down on his stomach with his ear close to the creek and listened.

After a while there was a tiny splash. Michael raised his head and saw a frog swimming from a rock across to the other shore. Something plopped just inside the shade of the trees. A pinecone rolled down the path and stopped, nestling among other fallen cones.

Movement flickered at the corner of Michael's eye, and he turned his head carefully. A little chipmunk dashed out from behind a tree. He stopped, holding his paws in front of his chest, and looked at Michael.

Slowly Michael reached into his pocket and brought out a squashed bit of roll left from lunch. He held it out toward the chipmunk. The chipmunk flicked his tail and came closer. His feet twinkled in quick little rushes. He came right up to Michael and looked at him with his brave, bright eyes. Michael didn't move. The chipmunk dashed to his fingers, snatched the roll, and skittered away. At the base of a tree, he stopped and nibbled on the crust.

A bird chirped from the tree overhead. The wind moved through the pine needles, and they shivered and sighed delicately together. Michael sat with his back against a tree trunk, contented, quiet. He listened to the small sounds around him.

Suddenly the silence was ended. *Honk honk! Beep beep! Vroom Vroom!* A procession of cars came tearing around the corner and raced toward him in clouds of dust. Hands waved out the windows. Kids' heads and dogs' heads hung out together, shouting and yelping.

"Michael! Hey, Michael!"

"Woof woof."

"Meoww."

"Ball four."

The McBrides and Camerons were coming back after him.

His mother jumped out of the car almost before it stopped. She raced toward him and scooped him up in her arms. "Michael, honey, we didn't mean to leave you. Everyone thought you were riding with someone else. Oh, it must have been awful for you."

"No," he said. "It was nice."

Dad and Kevin jumped out of the car. Kevin grabbed him away from his mother and set him astride his shoulders. He galloped around in a circle, yelling, "Michael's back. We got Michael back."

Timothy ran along beside him, making his motorcycle noises. Chipper fell out the back window of the car and chased after them, barking. Great-Aunt Olivia trotted along behind, trying to pat Michael on the shoulder and shrieking, "Oh, Matthew. It was all my fault. I thought Michael was you."

Hey, they really missed me, Michael thought. There're so many of them, but they still miss one little kid. I guess they do know I'm here, after all. That's nice, too.

They piled into the cars and went home. From then on, they always counted each other very carefully before they left on a trip, and they counted after every stop, just to make sure no one was lost again.

Michael yelled and thumped and giggled with the rest of them. But every so often, when he felt the need, he went off by himself. He found a private corner, sat there very quietly all alone, and listened to the small sounds of life.

The Big Tomato Smash

"Hurry, Michael," Mother called. "They're here."

Michael jammed his foot into his tennis shoe and ran downstairs with the laces flopping. His mother was on her knees in the living room, peering under the big green chair.

"Where is that cat?" she muttered. "Michael, have you seen Midnight?"

"Nope," he said, and sat down in the middle of the floor to tie his shoe. A sudden silence fell in the yard as his brother Kevin shut off the lawn mower. The front door opened, and Grandma McBride put her head in.

"Good morning, Michael, my love," she said cheerfully. "Where is your mother?"

"Behind the couch," he said.

Grandma McBride went into the living room just as Mom came crawling out backward. "What have you lost, Carol?"

"The cat," she said. "I know he's in the house someplace. I've got to put him out before we go. The last time that I left him inside while we were gone he did something awful under Heather's bed."

"Have you called him?" asked Grandma.

"He never comes when he's called. We'll have to find him. Michael, you look upstairs—under the beds, in the closets—everywhere. Connie, you check the cellar. Be sure to look on all the shelves."

"Can't we just close the cellar door?" Connie asked.

"Sure," Mom said, "if you'll agree to clean up anything that Midnight might do while we're gone."

Connie went to the cellar. Michael ran back upstairs. He looked under his bed, in his toybox, in his closet. He looked in and under everything in all the rooms. He found a lot of things, but not the cat. When he went back downstairs, Kevin had come inside with their cousin Barbara and Great-Aunt Olivia. They were looking for Midnight, too.

"There he is," cried Barbara. "I see his tail sticking out right there."

"That's Muffin's tail, you bean brain," said Kevin with disgust. "Can't you tell a dog from a cat?"

"How did that dog get back in?" Mom said. "Put her out in the backyard, Connie, and make sure the gate is closed."

"I have to do everything," Connie complained. "Why doesn't Michael ever do anything?"

"I *am* doing something. I'm looking for Midnight," Michael yelled. He stomped out to the TV room and opened the big basket that held

Mom's knitting. Once Midnight had been found sleeping in there, but today the basket was empty.

He stood in the middle of the room, thinking. If he were a cat, where would he hide? The dark cavern of the fireplace was in front of him. Two little golden sparks glowed inside. How could there still be sparks in the fireplace? They hadn't had a fire all summer.

Michael went closer and peered through the fire screen. Midnight lay there watching him, neatly curled up on the cold ashes, his chin resting on his paws. His dark coat was the same charcoal color as the ashes and the smoky bricks at the back. Only his round, shining eyes gave him away.

"I found him," Michael yelled. "He's in the fireplace." Michael pulled him out and lugged him to the back door. Little bits of ash and soot dropped off the cat's fur and drifted to the floor.

"In the fireplace, was he?" exclaimed Grandma McBride. "You're going to have barbecued cat one of these days."

Michael opened the screen door and pushed

Midnight over the threshold. Midnight pushed back. Chipper and Muffin jumped over the cat and bounced into the kitchen, wagging their tails.

Mom came charging in. "Get those animals out," she yelled. "Out! Out! *Out!*" She clapped her hands at them, and all three whirled and scuttled outside. She slammed the door. "Okay, kids. Get in the car. We want to go to the farm and buy the tomatoes before it gets hot."

"Let me drive, Mom," said Kevin. "I need the practice."

"Not now," she said. "But you can drive later today."

Kevin scowled. "I can drive practically as good as Mom," he mumbled into Michael's ear as they got into the backseat.

Michael didn't think that was true, but he didn't argue with him. Sometimes it was best to leave Kevin alone when he was in a bad mood.

Before long they came to the lane that led to the farm. A painted sign hung on the gatepost. *Pearson's. Farm Fresh Eggs. Dressed Fryers. Fruit and Vegetables in Season.* A square piece of cardboard was tacked on below. It announced in big, crooked red letters, *Special. Tomatoes.*

"Ummm, nothing like good fresh tomatoes," said Great-Aunt Olivia.

"And homemade chili sauce and tomato relish," said Grandma McBride.

Barbara giggled into Michael's ear. "Did you see the sign that said dressed fryers? What do chickens wear when they're dressed?"

"Dresses, of course." Michael started to laugh. "And blue jeans. And tennis shoes."

"Raincoats and hats," cried Connie.

"And pajamas," yelled Barbara.

"Overalls and aprons," shrieked Michael.

"Shhh, not so loud," said Mom, but she was laughing, too.

Kevin looked out the window with a bored expression on his face.

"Look at all the cars," said Mom. "I hope there's room to park." She guided the station wagon carefully between the cars that were parked every which way on the hard-packed dirt beside the field.

"Watch the ditch," said Kevin.

"Oh, Carol, look out for that deep ditch," Great-Aunt Olivia chimed in.

Mom stopped the car and firmly set the emergency brake. "Here we are, safe and sound. Now let's hurry and get our tomatoes while there are still some left."

They all walked over to the big, open shed. Bushels of ripe tomatoes were set out on wooden tables, along with corn, plums, peaches, green beans, radishes, watermelons, and cartons of eggs. They wandered up and down for some time, looking at the fruits and vegetables. Michael began to get bored.

"These tomatoes are almost too ripe," Mom whispered. "We should have come last week."

"It won't matter. We're going to cook them up right away. At this low price, we can afford to throw away a few. We'll start with this bushel of tomatoes, Mr. Pearson," Grandma McBride said to the man behind the cash register.

"Kevin, carry them to the car, please," Mom said. "Here are the keys to unlock the tailgate.

29

And set the basket down gently. Some of the tomatoes are a little soft."

Michael followed Kevin as he lugged the basket to the parking area. A blue car had its front bumper right up against the back of the station wagon. Behind it was another car. A cranky-looking woman got out and stood with her hands on her hips, looking at the two cars.

"Open the back door," Kevin said to Michael. "I'll have to set the tomatoes on the seat until she moves."

"Is this your car?" the woman asked. "Would you pull up so I can get out? And hurry! I'm late as it is."

"Sure," said Kevin, and he jumped behind the wheel.

"Better get Mom," said Michael.

"I can do it," said Kevin, giving him a fierce mind-your-own-business-if-you-know-what's-good-for-you look. "Besides, Mom said I could drive later. And it's later."

Kevin was fifteen and too old for Michael to argue with. He hopped into the backseat beside the tomatoes. Kevin started the engine and edged the station wagon forward a few inches.

"I can't pull straight ahead," he muttered. "I'll run in the ditch. I'll have to back up a little and then pull to the side."

He shifted into reverse. A horn blared behind him.

"Take it easy, lady. I know you're there."

He changed gears, and the station wagon crept slowly forward. Michael saw a dime lying on the floor of the car, and he got down on his knees to pick it up. Kevin shifted again, and the station wagon moved backward. The horn blasted, long and loud, as if the woman was leaning on it. Kevin made an angry sound and jammed the shift into drive.

The station wagon leaped ahead, and there was a big jolt as the front end dropped into the ditch. The basket toppled forward, and tomatoes bounced all over Michael, who was still on the floor. The extra-ripe ones split as they hit him. Red juicy pulp oozed out, over his head, neck, and back. Some rolled on the floor and squashed under his hands and knees. Juice dripped into his eyes, and he tried to wipe it away with a messy hand. All he did was smear more red pulp over his face.

Kevin was saying words Michael knew he shouldn't be saying. "Are you all right, Mikie?" He sounded scared. He hadn't called him Mikie for a long time.

"Yeah," Michael said. "But the tomatoes aren't."

He opened the car door with a sticky hand and half fell out into the ditch. Great-Aunt Olivia was standing at the top of the ditch, looking down at him. Her mouth dropped open, and her eyes stretched wide and round behind her glasses. He tried to scramble up toward her. His foot slipped on a tomato, and he fell on his face.

He heard a sort of scuffling noise, and Great-Aunt Olivia came sliding gently down into the ditch. She stopped in a heap beside him. Her eyes were closed. She had fainted.

His mother came next, wide-awake. She quickly examined Michael and Kevin and then turned to Great-Aunt Olivia. "It's all right, Aunt Olivia. Michael's not hurt. Neither is Kevin. The tomatoes

fell on Michael, that's all. Please wake up, Aunt Olivia."

Great-Aunt Olivia sat up groggily. "Squashed tomatoes," she said. "Is that all! I thought it was blood."

Everyone climbed out of the ditch. The woman in the blue car roared away in an angry cloud of dust. Mr. Pearson came with his tractor and pulled the station wagon out. It was hardly dented at all. They cleaned out the smashed tomatoes, and Mr. Pearson turned his garden hose on Michael to rinse him off. In a little while they were on their way home again with a new bushel of tomatoes in the cargo area.

"I'm really sorry, Mom," Kevin said for the fifth time. "I guess I'm not as good a driver as I thought. Will you ever let me drive again?"

"Don't even ask for a while," said Mom.

Great-Aunt Olivia was sitting in the backseat. She put her arm around Michael and hugged him. "You gave me such an awful fright, honey. You were so covered with tomatoes I couldn't even recognize my own dear little Matthew."

Michael sighed and looked at Kevin. Kevin looked away quickly, but it was too late. Michael started to giggle, and Kevin gave a funny snort that turned into a laugh. Mom, Barbara, Connie, and Grandma McBride started laughing, too. Great-Aunt Olivia looked puzzled for a minute; then she joined in. The station wagon hummed down the road, everybody crowded in together, and laughter spilled out all the windows.

The Thing in the Alley

It was one of those nights when almost everyone
had someplace to go. Mom and Dad were going
to a dinner that was for grown-ups only. Shawn
was taking his girl friend to a party. Kevin and
Heather had gone camping with Aunt Norma,
Uncle Jim, and the cousins: B. J., Becky, and
Walter. Timothy was spending the night with a

friend from school. Only Michael and Connie would be left at home. Grandma Cameron was coming to baby-sit with them.

"I don't like that word, *baby-sit*," Connie complained. She complained about a lot of things. In fact, Dad sometimes said that Connie worked at complaining as hard as if she were getting paid for it. If everybody had just one job they were supposed to do for the family, her job must be to find things wrong and complain about them so everyone else would notice them, too.

"Baby-sit was all right when I was little," she went on. "But I'm not a baby anymore. I'm nine years old. I don't need a baby-sitter."

"Neither do I," said Michael. "I'm almost eight, and I'm not a baby, either."

"Neither one of you is a baby," said Dad. "That's just a word that people get in the habit of saying. We start out using it when you kids really are babies, and we keep on. You grow up, but the word never does. Grandma Cameron is coming to keep you company. And you keep *her* company, so she doesn't have to be alone."

"Well, all right," Connie said generously. "If it's just for company."

The front door opened. "Hello, here we are," called Grandma Cameron.

Michael ran to meet her. "Hi, Grandma. Hi, Captain Kidd."

The parrot ruffled his feathers angrily and didn't speak. Grandma put him in a small cage when she took him out, and he didn't like it. He preferred the big cage he lived in at home.

"He's feeling grouchy," Grandma said. She put the cage on the dining-room table.

Mom came downstairs, in her new dress and with her hair in curls. Michael thought she looked pretty and strange at the same time, as though she were somebody else and not his everyday Mom.

"Here's the phone number where we'll be." She handed Grandma Cameron a slip of paper. "Be sure to call if you have a problem."

"We won't have any problems," Grandma said. "Everything will be just fine." She yawned widely. "Excuse me. I was up late last night."

"Reading murder mysteries, I'll bet," said Mom.

"You know I just love the horrible things," said Grandma. "I didn't intend to read the whole book, but once I got started it was so exciting that I couldn't stop. I stayed up until I finished it. You might like it, Carol. It's called *The Empty Grave*."

"Sounds scary," said Mom.

"Oh, it was. I loved it," said Grandma.

"Tell us about it," cried Michael.

"It's time for us to go. We don't want to be late," said Dad. He kissed Michael and Connie good-bye, and so did Mom.

Their car drove away, and Grandma yawned again. "I am *so* sleepy. Why did I stay up so late when I knew I was coming over here tonight?"

"Tell us about the murder," said Michael again. "I want to hear about the empty grave." Even as he spoke, he wasn't sure he really did want to hear about it. That was the way with scary things: he thought he wanted to hear about them, and then when he did, sometimes he was sorry.

"No," said Grandma. "I brought another book to read to you. It's called *Nobody Is Perfick*."

Connie looked at the cover. *"Perfick* is spelled wrong."

Grandma smiled. "Aren't you a smart little girl? Come sit beside me on the couch so you can see the pictures."

Michael sat on one side and Connie on the other. Grandma began reading:

> "Say something nice.
> " 'Lizards.'
> "That's not nice."

The book was funny, and Connie and Michael giggled all the way through it. Grandma giggled, too, but she kept stopping every few pages to yawn.

"Read some more," said Michael, when the book was finished.

Grandma rubbed her eyes. "This time you kids can read to me. I have to rest my eyes for a minute." She lay down on the couch, and Connie ran off to find one of her books to read.

"Don't go to sleep, Grandma," she said, when she came back.

"I'm only closing my eyes. I'll get up when you

finish reading, and we'll have some ice cream."

Connie read, Michael listened, and Grandma rested her eyes. Captain Kidd squawked and rustled around in his cage in the other room.

After a while, Connie said, "The end," and closed the book. "How was that, Grandma Cameron?"

Grandma gave a little snore.

"She's asleep," said Michael. "She's been asleep since page ten."

Connie giggled. "I read Grandma a bedtime story."

"Ball four. Ball four," Captain Kidd yelled. He flapped his wings and scuffled his feet. Michael walked out to look at him. The parrot grabbed the cage door with his claw and rattled it.

"I'll let him out for a minute," said Michael. He opened the door, and Captain Kidd hopped out onto the table. He preened a little, and then he flapped around the room. He lit on the back of a chair.

Yip. Yip. Yap. Chipper and Muffin were at the back door, barking to be let in. Connie opened the door.

"Take a walk," Captain Kidd cried, and suddenly, before Michael knew what was happening, he darted over Connie's head and flew out the door.

"Close the door," Michael yelled, but it was too late.

"Shhh," Connie hissed. "Don't wake Grandma. She'll be mad. We'll get him back before she wakes up."

They ran outside. It was quite dark, and they couldn't see Captain Kidd anywhere. "Captain Kidd. Captain Kidd," they called.

"You're out," the parrot croaked from somewhere over the fence.

"He's in Parker's yard." They climbed over the fence. Behind them, Chipper and Muffin whined and yelped at being left inside.

"Come here, Captain Kidd. Come back."
Silence.

"Where are you? We've got a cracker for you," called Connie.

"That's a lie," said Michael.

"He doesn't know. We'll give him one when we get him in the house."

"There he is on the fence," said Michael. They

went slowly across the darkened yard. "Nice Captain Kidd. Come on home. Grandma Cameron will miss you."

The bird watched them come. When they were almost up to him, he darted away over the fence.

"Oh, darn and blast," Connie cried. "Now he's out in the alley."

They scrambled over that fence, too. Chipper and Muffin howled and cried dismally behind them. It was shadowy in the lane between the houses. Bushes, trees, and high fences darkened the alley, looming close on both sides. All the houses had their backs turned, seeming shut and secret and far away, not looking behind them where the children walked.

Everything was very different tonight. Michael felt as though he was in some strange place where he had never been before. He thought of the book that Grandma read—*The Empty Grave*. She hadn't wanted to tell them about it because it was about murder. Something awful happened in the book, and she didn't want them to know. Books were true, sometimes.

He looked over his shoulder. He'd never noticed before that the alley was so long. There was a little curve with thick bushes leaning over so he couldn't see the other end. The lane closed in behind them, and their house seemed far away, no lights visible, lost in the black night. The dogs were quiet. There wasn't any noise at all, except a sort of listening silence, as though something was waiting to happen.

He reached his hand toward Connie, and their fingers locked together. He could tell by the tight way her hand gripped his that she was afraid, too. They walked slowly along the middle of the alley, taking small, quiet steps, almost on tiptoe.

Michael was sure the book that Grandma Cameron read was about a real murder. If the grave was empty, maybe whatever had been in the grave was out walking around. It probably came from the old cemetery over on Pine Street, only a few blocks away. They were heading right toward there. Every step they took was one step nearer to the graveyard and the thing that came through the dark night streets, looking for them.

It came closer and closer, swinging its dark head from side to side, sniffing, like an animal.

"Captain Kidd," Connie whispered.

"Be quiet!" Michael jerked at her hand. "It'll hear you."

She didn't even have to ask what "it" was that would hear them. She *knew*.

"Let's go back," Connie whispered. "We'll get Grandma Cameron."

Before they could turn, they heard something in the shadows ahead of them. There was a soft scrabbling sound, like padded feet, shuffling quietly in the dirt. Something was breathing, panting almost, in the darkness ahead of them. A heavy shape came slowly toward them, and Michael could see the faint shine of light on glittering eyes.

His legs were paralyzed, rooted to the ground like old tree stumps.

"Run," Connie squeaked, but before they could move there was a sudden flapping in the tree above them.

"Strike three," squalled the harsh voice of Captain Kidd. He came down out of the tree like an eagle and dive-bombed the horrible thing in

the alley. He beat his wings over the dark head, and the shape gave a frightened yelp, turned, and fled away. At the end of the lane, it stopped and looked back. They could see it plainly in the glow from the streetlights at the end of the block.

"It's only a dog," Michael said with a gasp. "That big black dog that lives on Cedar Street."

The parrot lit on Connie's shoulder with a smug little squawk. "Captain Kidd, you saved us," she said.

"Do you suppose he knew it was a dog?" asked Michael. "Or do you think he thought it was something else?"

"Well, he doesn't like strange dogs," said Connie. "But maybe he can't see in the dark any better than we can. Anyway, he's a brave parrot."

They took him home and put him in his cage again. He didn't seem to mind but settled in contentedly, nibbling at the cracker he held in one claw.

Grandma Cameron suddenly sat up on the couch. "Oh, my. I must have dozed off for a minute. Let's have our ice cream now. Are you kids feeding that bird again? You're spoiling him."

"He deserves it. He's a good parrot," Connie said.

Grandma took out the ice cream and scooped it into bowls. "We've had such a nice, quiet evening. I told your mother we wouldn't have any problems."

"No problems," Michael and Connie said together, laughing.

"You're out," chortled Captain Kidd, and he winked one wise, round eye.

Mold and Magnets

"Hey, Michael, have you seen the volleyball anywhere?" Timothy yelled, as he clumped into the kitchen.

"No." Michael stood by the refrigerator, moving around the magnets that were attached to the door. Some were black and shaped like tiny cast-iron skillets, pans, and irons. Others were little glass mounds with seeds inside—corn, peas, beans, and watermelon.

Each magnet held a piece of paper, so the door of the refrigerator was almost covered with notes and reminders. There was a grocery list, a clipping from the newspaper telling about a new exhibit at the museum, a note scratched in big red letters that said, *Matthew's Birthday*!!, a sheet of paper listing the chores that each McBride was supposed to do during the week, and a postcard from the veterinarian warning that Chipper and Muffin needed their rabies shots again.

"Come and help me look. Kevin wants the volleyball and net," Timothy said bossily.

Michael shook his head.

"Come on. You're not doing anything important."

"Yes, I am," Michael said. "I'm waiting."

"What are you waiting for?"

"He's waiting for me to finish the sloppy-joe sauce," Heather said, coming in from the pantry with some cans of tomato sauce. "He wants to taste it."

"Aghhh." Timothy clutched his throat and staggered around the kitchen. "It'll kill you."

"I'm hungry," Michael said.

Timothy lifted the lid and peered into the pot in which the hamburger and onions were simmering. "I've got a deal for you, Michael. You go ahead and taste it. Then we'll wait five minutes, and if you don't throw up, I'll eat some, too."

Michael snickered. Heather turned her back and looked haughtily at the wall as she stirred the hamburger.

Kevin and Connie came into the kitchen. "Come on," Kevin said to Timothy. "You're supposed to be looking for the volleyball."

"I want to play, too," Michael said, but nobody heard him.

"I thought for sure it was in the garage," Timothy said.

"Nope. Maybe it's upstairs."

They clattered up to their rooms, and Michael trailed along behind. He watched from the door as Kevin looked around in the room he shared with Shawn. He looked in the closet and behind the beds and furniture. They heard Timothy crashing around in his and Michael's room across the hall.

"I want to play volleyball, too," Michael said again, but Kevin brushed past him without seeming to hear and went into the other room. Michael followed and sat on his bed.

"Why is everything such a mess? It's impossible to find anything," Timothy grumbled, and he kicked at a pile of shoes and clothes lying on the floor.

"Your side of the room is messier than mine," Michael said.

This time Kevin heard him. "You're right," he agreed. "Timothy is the worst. The rest of us may not be very neat, but Timothy's half is always a total disaster area. Just look at this." He picked up a goldfish bowl that was stuffed full of socks and underwear. "Is this any place to keep your dirty laundry?"

"Well, the fish died."

"Before or after you put in those socks?"

Connie flopped on her stomach and started dragging things out from under Timothy's bed. "Look here. More rotten socks, a Frisbie, books, an apple core, old school papers, kite string . . . yuk!" She squealed and jumped to her knees, wiping her hand on her jeans.

"What's wrong?" asked Kevin.

"Ughh, there's something really awful under there, all soft and squishy."

Kevin and Timothy got down on their knees and peered under the bed. "Oh, gross! What is it?"

Michael tried to squeeze in, but there wasn't room.

"Don't touch it. Maybe it's alive."

"Not anymore. It looks like a dead rat."

Michael finally wiggled in so he could see under the bed. There was a large, gray, furry patch of something. "I've never seen anything like it before," he said.

"Not many people have." Kevin poked at it cautiously with a pencil. A little glob of yellow stuck on the sharp lead as he pulled it back. He held it at arm's length and squinted at it.

"I know what it is," Timothy cried. "It's cheese. That's my cheese-and-salami sandwich."

Kevin groaned. "Timothy, you are the world's worst! How could you be so dumb and let a sandwich lie under there until it died?"

"Remember how I used to wake up every night because I was so hungry? That sandwich was my reserve snack. For some reason I didn't wake up anymore, and I forgot it was there."

"If Mom sees it, she'll have a fit. Get busy and clean it up."

Timothy got busy, complaining all the while. "How did it get so far back under the bed? I left it right near the edge?"

"It probably crawled back. A hairy sandwich could do almost anything, even crawl around."

Michael and Connie lay on their stomachs, watching. "You missed some," Connie said.

"Oh, I got most of it. I'll get the rest after we play volleyball."

"You'll forget," said Kevin. "And another mold monster will start growing, even bigger and fiercer than this one. It will crawl up on your bed in the night and smother you." He made a growling noise and put his hands over Timothy's face.

Timothy pushed them away. "Knock it off. I just remembered where the volleyball is. Mom put it out in the shed when she had her last attack of clean-up-itis."

He and Kevin ran downstairs, with Michael pounding after them. Timothy took the storage-shed key from the drawer and went out the side door.

"Gimme the key. I'll unlock the shed." Kevin grabbed at the key, and Timothy jerked his hand back. The key fell onto the porch with a clink and disappeared down a wide crack.

"Now look what you've done!"

They got on their knees and peered down the crack.

"I see it, right there," Kevin said.

"Yeah, but we can't reach it."

Heather and Connie came out onto the porch.

"Isn't there a crawl space under there?"

"Not right there. Remember when Mom dropped her pearl birthday earring through the same crack? Dad had to pry up a couple of boards."

"Get the crowbar," said Timothy.

"He'll be mad if we tear up the porch," said Kevin.

"He'll also be mad if we lose the key to the shed."

"What you need is a magnet on a string," said Heather.

"The key isn't iron. It's aluminum or something funny like that," said Timothy.

"The key chain is steel," said Kevin. "Where's a magnet?"

"On the refrigerator," said Michael.

"Oh, those magnets are too little," said Kevin. "Besides, they're such funny shapes. We couldn't hook them onto anything."

"We could tie them on a yardstick," said Michael, but nobody paid any attention, as usual.

"How about my gum? We could put that on a yardstick and poke it down," suggested Connie.

"Good idea," said Kevin. "Get the yardstick."

Timothy ran off, and Connie chomped her gum to get it good and sticky. They stuck it on the end of the yardstick and poked it down the crack.

"A little to the left," said Heather, squinting

down the crack. "Oh, you missed. Try again. No, too far. Right there. Good, you got it. No, wait. The key fell off. Try again, straight down. No, it's not sticking. You jabbed the gum in the dirt too many times. It's so covered with dirt there's no room for the chain to stick."

"Hey, you lost my gum," Connie complained.

"Do you really want it back? It's full of dirt."

"I guess not. I'll chew some more, and we'll try again." She ran up to her room to get more gum.

Michael went to the kitchen and took three round magnets off the refrigerator door. He lined them up on the kitchen counter and tried to think of something to hold them together, something that the magnets could work through, something like cloth. He looked in Mom's sewing supplies and saw some pink nylon net left from one of Heather's dance costumes.

He had seen Mom cut little squares of netting and put the remains of soap bars inside. She fastened the bundle shut with a Twist-em from a bread bag and used up all the little leftover pieces of soap. Maybe he could do the same thing with magnets.

He cut a small piece of netting and lined up the magnets in the middle. When he tried to tie the netting shut, the magnets slipped around in a jumble. He needed something to hold them in a straight row.

Connie ran down the hall, noisily chewing some fresh gum.

"Hurry up," yelled Timothy.

"Wait a minute. I just started chewing. It's not sticky enough yet."

Michael found a piece of cardboard and cut it about the same length and width as the three magnets. He laid it on top of them and bent it in the middle to hold the magnets. It looked like a little roof. Then carefully he folded the ends of the net over the package and secured them with a Twist-em. It wasn't tight enough, and when he picked it up, everything fell apart. He started over.

He could hear the others yelling on the porch.

"It's not going to stick. Connie, you didn't chew long enough."

"It's not my fault. I would have chewed longer, but you practically snatched the gum out of my mouth. I almost bit you."

"Then I'd have to get a rabies shot like Chipper and Muffin," said Timothy.

"Oh, shut up, you two," said Kevin. "This isn't going to work, anyway. Didn't Shawn have a horseshoe magnet for one of his science projects? That should pick up the chain. Let's look for it. It might be upstairs or down in the cellar."

The kids scampered down the hall and clattered up and down the stairs like a herd of goats.

Michael put the cardboard roof on the magnets again and tied them tight in a little row inside the netting. He took a roll of transparent tape and went to the porch. He put the row of magnets on the end of the yardstick, pulled the netting up the sides, and taped it snugly.

Carefully he slid the stick through the crack. He lay on his stomach and moved it around until the end was right over the key

chain. He pressed down gently and then lifted. The key and the chain dangled on the end. He pulled it up slowly. It got as far as the crack and dropped off when it scraped against the boards. He attached it again and drew it up again. This time he was able to slide the key through the crack.

Footsteps drummed across the floor, and the older kids ran back to the porch.

"It's not my fault we can't find the magnet," Timothy yelled. "The dumb thing is probably locked in the shed with the volleyball."

"Nobody can ever find anything in this house," Kevin yelled back. "What we need is some organization."

"I've got the key," Michael said.

"Michael," Kevin shouted at him. "Why are you just sitting there like a lump? Get up and help us find the magnet."

"I've got the key," Michael said again.

In the sudden silence everybody looked at Michael, the key, and the yardstick contraption.

"Look at that," Kevin said. "Michael, you're a genius."

"Thanks," he said modestly.

"Why didn't you tell us what you were going to do? We would have helped you."

"I tried to, but nobody would listen. As usual."

"Hey, you guys," Kevin said. "He's right. We always ignore him and talk over the top of him just because he's the littlest. But he's got some good ideas. From now on, everybody listens to Michael. Right?"

"Right!" they all shouted. "We'll listen to Michael."

Michael smiled. Having his bigger brothers and sisters say he was important, too, made him feel good. From now on, they would know he was there even if he was the littlest and even if they still yelled over the top of his head sometimes. Maybe he couldn't be the center of attention every day, but nobody would ever really forget Michael again.